Lionel
The Lonely Monster

Fred BLunT

OXFORD
UNIVERSITY PRESS

Lionel the monster found it hard to make friends.
You see, children were frightened of Lionel
because he was a monster ...

. . . and grown ups were too busy to notice him.

Lionel was feeling lonely. Lonely and sad.

So sad, he had a little cry.

Boo Hoo Hoo Hoo

A passing dog stopped to give
the monster a concerned prod
and a friendly lick.

Then it brought him a stick.

Lionel had never played fetch before . . .

. . . and the little dog had never had a stick thrown so far before!

Fetch turned into
hide-and-seek
and . . .

. . . hide-and-seek soon turned into chase . . .

. . . all the way to the **playground**.

Lionel had never

had so much fun!

The new friends were relaxing under a tree, when Lionel noticed the dog looked rather sad.

Whatever could the matter be?

But then he spotted it—a poster for a missing dog called Milo.

Lionel checked the name on his friend's collar and sure enough it read MILO.

Lionel didn't know what to do.
He had only just made friends
with Milo and didn't want
to lose him now.

But he knew someone
would be missing
Milo, and he must be
missing them too.

So Lionel did the right thing and took Milo home, to the address on his collar.

Nervously, he pressed the doorbell and quickly headed back up the garden path.

Lionel didn't want to **scare** anyone.

A little girl opened the door
and *squealed* with delight
when she saw her dog.

But then she spotted Lionel and screamed

Lionel turned to see the terrified
girl pointing at him.

Lionel was used to children being
scared of him, but somehow it
hurt more this time.

But Milo was barking frantically as Lionel walked away.

He shot off after him, followed by the girl shouting "STOP!"

Lionel turned . . .

. . . and Milo **leapt** into his
arms, licking his face all over.

That's when the girl realised . . .

. . . it was the
monster who had
returned her dog!

She introduced herself as Lucy and asked
Lionel if he wanted to be friends.

Then she dragged him off home to play.

Together they played
dressing up . . .

. . . dollies . . .

. . . and hide-and-seek.

When it was time for Lionel to go home, Lucy made him promise they would be **Best Friends Forever.**

And then she surprised him,
with a **Great-Big-Hug**.

From that day on,
Lionel was never lonely again.

The end